Oh, Harry!

For Yann—M.K.

For my Emily. My Sparky, the light within my light.—B.M.

The illustrator thanks Suzanne Payne, director of the Equestrian Center at Smith College,
and her staff for their help in the preparation of these images.
Thanks to Maxine Kumin for allowing my assistant and me to photograph her barn
and her horse, Deuteronomy, may he rest in peace;
to Cara Moser for her help in matters photographic and equine;
to Jackson Harper for posing as the brat.

Library of Congress Cataloging-in-Publication Data

Kumin, Maxine, 1925–
  Oh, Harry! / Maxine Kumin ; illustrated by Barry Moser. — 1st ed.
    p. cm.
  "A Neal Porter Book."
  Summary: Harry the Horse excels at calming skittish equines in Adams & Son's show-horse barn, but he
faces a different challenge when mischievous six-year-old Algernon Adams the Third arrives.
  ISBN 978-1-59643-439-4 (alk. paper)
  [1. Stories in rhyme. 2. Horses—Fiction. 3. Behavior—Fiction.] I. Moser, Barry, ill. II. Title.

PZ8.3.K95Oh 2011
[E]—dc22
                                                                                    2010024837

Roaring Brook Press books are available for special promotions and premiums.
For details contact: Director of Special Markets, Holtzbrinck Publishers.

First Edition 2011
Book design by Jennifer Browne
Printed in March 2011 in China
by South China Printing Co. Ltd., Dongguan City, Guangdong Province

1 3 5 7 9 8 6 4 2

Oh, Harry!

Maxine Kumin ★ *Illustrated by* Barry Moser

2010 9909 1

A NEAL PORTER BOOK
ROARING BROOK PRESS
NEW YORK

Harry the Horse was a homely sort.
His ears were long and his neck was short.

His hooves were as thick as a telephone book
And when he trotted, the sidewalk shook.

In the show-horse barn of Adams & Son
Harry the Horse was the only one

Who wasn't elegant, slim, and tall,
Who didn't jitter and pace the stall

Or prance and paw or come up to the gate
In a terrible mood and rear up straight.

Not good old Harry, the easygoing.
His eye was kind. He was calm and knowing

And the trainer loved him. He loved the way
Harry could comfort the wildest bay

Or trot alongside a nervous filly
And keep her from doing anything silly.

He didn't exactly have his own stall.
Whenever they took in an animal

Who was fancy and green and young and new
They'd put Harry next door. He knew what to do.

He'd lean down over the topmost rail
And nuzzle the newcomer calm, without fail.

If all of the stalls were full for a while
Harry was free to live in the aisle.

And the show-horse barn of Adams & Son
Was a happy barn until Algernon

Adams the Third, at the age of six,
Arrived with his bag of horrendous tricks.

He ran with a war whoop up and down
In spite of the trainer's angry frown.

He climbed to the hayloft with an umbrella
Till the trainer ordered, "Get down, young fella!"

So he hopped back down and opened it wide
With a whoosh in the face of the stable's pride

And joy, a mare named May Queen Daisy
Who shivered and shook and nearly went crazy.

He hid behind doors. He shouted "Boo!"
As each of the horses was led through.

But one day fate paid Algie a trick.
He climbed in the grain bin. The lid went click!

And there was the Bad Boy out of sight
Locked up, so far as he knew, for the night.

It was getting dark. The trainer had gone.
The horses, all fed, were beginning to yawn.

The barn was so still you could surely have heard
A mouse squeak . . . or Algernon Adams the Third.

Luckily, Harry was loose in the aisle
When Algie fell in. He smiled a smile.

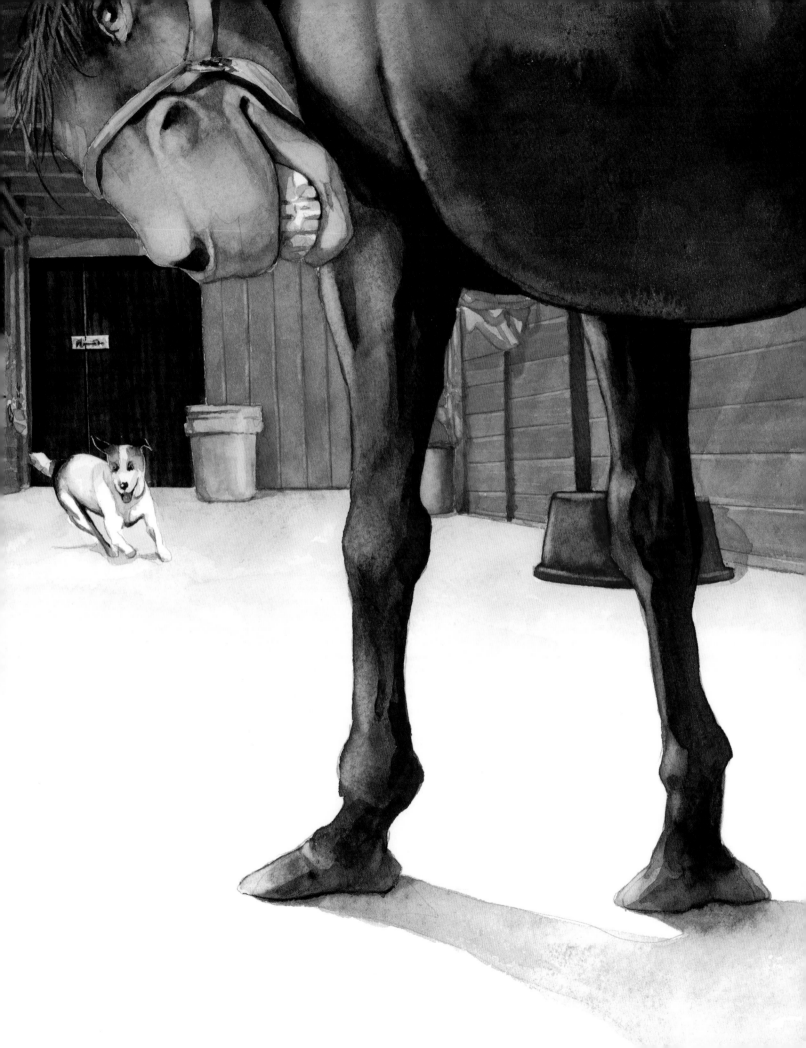

A remarkable thing about homely old Harry:
The tip of his nose was extraordinary.

The trainer had seen him snuffle around
In a box of cereal O's he'd found.

He could use his nose like a human hand
To extract one O at a time on demand.

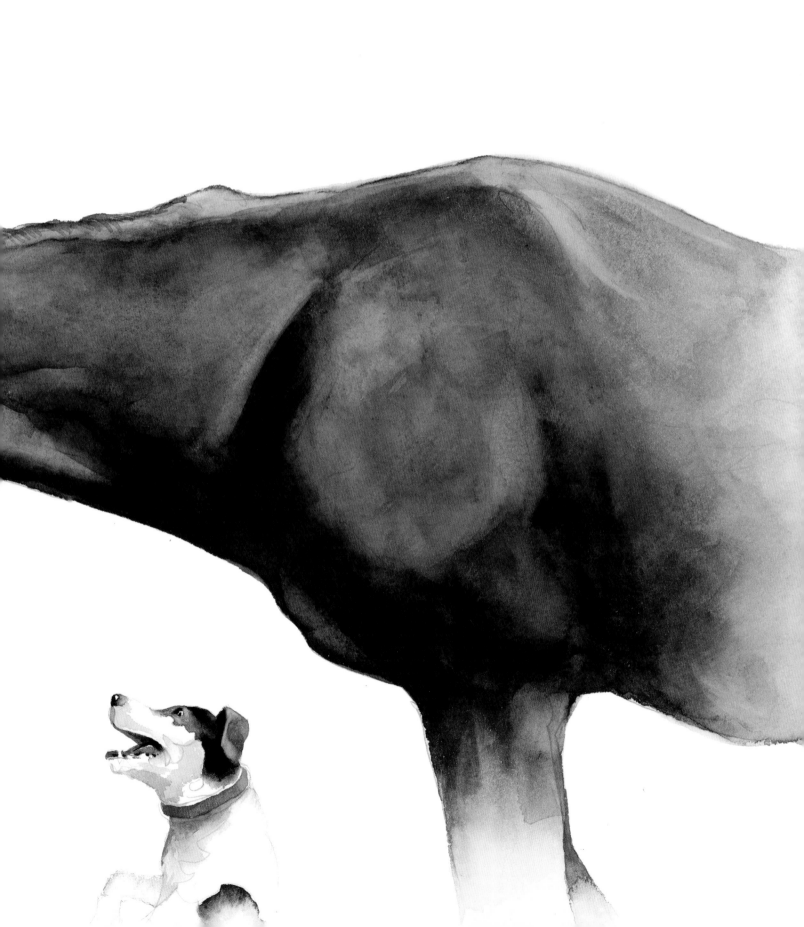

Harry could open the lids of pots.
He could undo latches and untie knots.

There wasn't a bolt he couldn't slide
Including the one with Algie inside.

So after he thought that the little dear
Was tired of yelling, "Lemme out of here!"

Harry ambled across the floor
And slid the bolt on the grain-room door.

He studied the dangerous wooden bin
Algernon was a prisoner in

And using the very tip of his muzzle
He finally managed to open the puzzle.

He picked Algie up by the back of his shirt
(He used his front teeth so it didn't hurt).

But before he set Algie down again
Harry shook him to dust off the grain.

Next morning the stable buzzed, "Have you heard
The news about Algernon Adams the Third?

He's a different child! So calm, so polite!
He must have slept next to Harry last night!"

And Harry wrinkled his muzzle to show
He knew all about Algie there was to know

As he quietly nibbled a cereal O.